DAEDALUS A

KING MIDAS

For Francesca

DAEDALUS AND ICARUS

ICARUS

KING MIDAS

GERALDINE M^cCAUGHREAN
ILLUSTRATED BY TONY ROSS

ORCHARD BOOKS

ORCHARD BOOKS
96 Leonard Street, London EC2A 4RH
Orchard Books Australia
14 Mars Road, Lane Cove, NSW 2066
ISBN 1 86039 532 5 (paperback)
ISBN 1 86039 439 6 (hardback)
First published in Great Britain 1997
This edition published in 1998
Text © Geraldine McCaughrean 1992
Illustrations © Tony Ross 1997
1 2 3 4 5 6 02 01 00 99 98
The right of Geraldine McCaughrean to be identified as the author and
Tony Ross as the illustrator of this work has been asserted by them
in accordance with the Copyright, Designs and Patents Act, 1988.
A CIP catalogue record for this book is available
from the British Library.
Printed in Great Britain.

DAEDALUS
AND
ICARUS

The island of Crete was ruled by King
Minos, whose reputation for
wickedness had spread to every shore.
One day he summoned to his country a
famous inventor named Daedalus.
"Come, Daedalus, and bring your son,
Icarus, too. I have a job for you,
and I pay well."

King Minos wanted Daedalus to build him a palace, with soaring towers and a high, curving roof. In the cellars there was to be a maze of many corridors—so twisting and dark that any man who once ventured in there would never find his way out again.

"What is it for?" asked Daedalus. "Is it a treasure vault? Is it a prison to hold criminals?"

But Minos only replied, "Build my labyrinth as I told you, I pay you to build, not to ask questions."

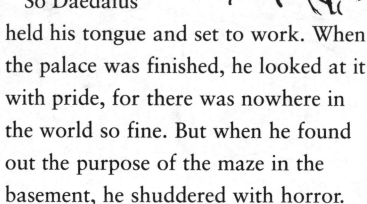

So Daedalus held his tongue and set to work. When the palace was finished, he looked at it with pride, for there was nowhere in the world so fine. But when he found out the purpose of the maze in the basement, he shuddered with horror.

For at the heart of that maze, King Minos put a beast—a thing too horrible to describe. He called it the Minotaur, and he fed it on men and women!

Then Daedalus wanted to leave Crete at once, and forget both maze and Minotaur. So he went to King Minos to ask for his money.

"I regret," said King Minos, "I cannot let you leave Crete, Daedalus. You are the only man who knows the secret of the maze and how to escape from it. The secret must never leave this island. So I'm afraid I must keep you and Icarus here a while longer."

"How much longer?" gasped Daedalus.

"Oh—just until you die," replied Minos cheerfully. "But never mind. I have plenty of work for a man as clever as you."

Daedalus and Icarus lived in great comfort in King Minos' palace. But they lived the life of prisoners. Their rooms were in the tallest palace tower, with beautiful views across the island. They ate delectable food and wore expensive clothes. But at night the door of their fine apartment was locked, and a guard stood outside. It was a comfortable prison, but it was a prison even so. Daedalus was deeply unhappy.

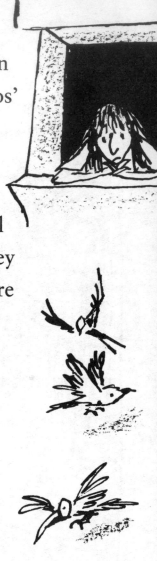

Every day he put seed out on the window sill, for the birds. He liked to study their brilliant colours, the clever overlapping of their feathers, the way they soared on the sea wind. It comforted him to think that they at least were free to come and go. The birds had only to spread their wings and they could leave Crete behind them, whereas Daedalus and Icarus must stay for ever in their luxurious cage.

Young Icarus could not understand his father's unhappiness. "But I like it here," he said. "The king gives us gold and this tall tower to live in."

Daedalus groaned. "But to work for such a wicked man, Icarus! And to be prisoners all our days ... We shan't stay. We shan't!"

"But we can't get away, can we!" said Icarus. "How can anybody escape from an island? Fly?" He snorted with laughter.

14

Daedalus did not answer. He scratched his head and stared out of the window at the birds pecking seed on the sill.

From that day onwards, he got up early each morning and stood at the open window. When a bird came for the seed, Daedalus begged it to spare him one feather. Then each night, when everyone else had gone to bed, Daedalus worked by candlelight on his greatest invention of all.

Early mornings. Late nights. A whole
year went by. Then one morning Icarus
was woken by his father shaking his
shoulder. "Get up, Icarus, and don't
make a sound. We are leaving Crete."

"But how? It's impossible!"

Daedalus pulled out a bundle from under his bed. "I've been making something, Icarus." Inside were four great folded fans of feathers. He stretched them out on the bed. They were wings! "I sewed the feathers together with strands of wool from my blanket. Now hold still."

Daedalus melted down a candle and daubed his son's shoulders with sticky wax. "Yes, I know it's hot, but it will soon cool." While the wax was still soft, he stuck two of the wings to Icarus' shoulder blades.

"Now you must help me put on my wings, Son. When the wax sets hard, you and I will fly away from here, as free as birds!"

"I'm scared!" whispered Icarus as he stood on the narrow window ledge, his knees knocking and his huge wings drooping down behind. The lawns and courtyards of the palace lay far below. The royal guards looked as small as ants. "This won't work!"

"Courage, son!" said Daedalus.
"Keep your arms out wide and fly close
to me. Above all—are you
listening, Icarus?"

"Y-y-yes, Father."

"Above all,
don't fly too high!
Don't fly too close
to the sun!"

"Don't fly too
close to the sun,"
Icarus repeated,
with his eyes tight
shut. Then he gave
a cry as his father
nudged him off
the window sill.

He plunged downwards. With a crack, the feathers behind him filled with wind, and Icarus found himself flying. Flying!

"I'm flying!" he crowed.

The little guards looked up in astonishment, and wagged their swords, and pointed and shouted, "Tell the king! Daedalus and Icarus are ... are ... flying away!"

By dipping first one wing, then the other, Icarus found that he could turn to the left and the right.

The wind tugged at his hair. His legs
trailed out behind him. He saw the
fields and streams as he had never seen
them before!

Then they were out over the sea.
The seagulls pecked at him angrily,
so Icarus flew higher, where they could
not reach him.

He copied their shrill cry and taunted
them: "You can't catch me!"

"Now remember, don't fly too high!"
called Daedalus, but his words were
drowned by the screaming of the gulls.

"I'm the first boy ever to fly! I'm
making history! I shall be famous!"
thought Icarus, as he flew up
and up higher and higher.

At last Icarus was looking the sun itself in the face. "Think you're the highest thing in the sky, do you?" he jeered. "I can fly just as high as you! higher, even!" He did not notice the drips of sweat on his forehead: he was so determined to out-fly the sun.

Soon its vast heat beat on his face
and on his back and on the great wings
stuck on with wax. The wax softened.
The wax trickled. The wax dripped.
One feather came unstuck. Then a
plume of feathers
fluttered slowly
down.

Icarus
stopped
flapping his
wings. His
father's
words came
back to him
clearly now:
"Don't fly too near to the sun!"

With a great
sucking noise, the
wax on his shoulders
came unstuck. Icarus
tried to catch hold of
the wings, but they
just folded up in his
hands. He plunged
down, his two fists
full of feathers—
down and down
and down.

The clouds did
not stop his fall.

The seagulls did
not catch him in
their beaks.

His own father could only watch as Icarus hurtled head first into the glittering sea and sank deep down among the sharks and eels and squid. And all that was left of proud Icarus was a litter of waxy feathers floating on the sea.

KING MIDAS

There was once a king called Midas who was almost as stupid as he was greedy.

When there was a music competition between the two gods Pan and Apollo, Midas was asked to be judge. Now Pan was Midas' friend, so instead of listening to the music to judge whose was best, he decided to let Pan win even before they began to play.

Comparing Apollo's music with Pan's is like comparing a golden trumpet with a tin whistle. But Midas had already made up his mind.

"Pan was the better! Oh definitely! No doubt about it. Pan was quite the better," he said. On and on he went, praising Pan, until Apollo turned quite scarlet with rage and pointed a magic finger at King Midas.

"There is something wrong with your ears if you think Pan's music is better than mine."

"Nothing's wrong with my ears," said foolish King Midas.

"Oh no? Well, we can soon change that!"

When he got home, Midas' ears were itching. He looked in the mirror and— horror of horrors!— his ears were growing. Longer and longer they grew, furrier and furrier, until he had brown and pink donkey's ears.

Midas found he could hide the ears if he crammed them both into a tall hat. "Nobody must see them," he thought as he walked about with his hat pulled down over his eyes. All day he wore it. He

even wore it at night, so that the queen would not see his ass's ears.

Nobody noticed. It was a great relief. They only saw that the king wore a tall hat all day long, and hurried to do the same, thinking it was the latest fashion.

But there was one person from whom Midas could not hide his secret. When the barber came to cut his hair, the dreadful truth came out.

The barber gasped. The barber stared. The barber stuffed a towel into his mouth to keep himself from laughing.

"You will tell no one!" commanded King Midas.

"Of course not! Never! No one! I promise!" babbled the barber, and cut the king's hair and helped him back on with his hat. It was to be their secret, never to be told.

The barber had given his promise. He never broke his promises. But oh dear! It was such a hard secret to keep! He ached to tell somebody. He would suddenly burst out laughing in public and could not explain why. He lay awake at nights, for fear of talking in his sleep. He kept that secret until he thought it would burn holes in him!

But at last he just had to tell it.

The barber took a very long walk, right away from town, all the way to the river. He dug a hole in the ground and put his head deep down it. Then he whispered into the hole, "King Midas has long ass's ears!"

After that he felt a lot better.

And the rain rained and the grass grew and the reeds by the river grew too.

Meanwhile, Midas (wearing his tall cap, of course) was walking in his garden when he met a satyr—half-man, half-horse. The satyr was lost. Midas gave him breakfast and directed him on his way.

"I'm so grateful," said the satyr. "Permit me to reward you. I shall grant you one wish."

He could have wished to be rid of his ass's ears, but no. At once Midas' head filled with pictures of money, wealth, treasure ... gold! His eyes glistened. "Oh please, please! Grant that everything I touch turns to gold!"

"Oof. Not a good idea," said the satyr. "Think again."

But Midas insisted. That was his wish. The satyr shrugged and went on his way.

"Huh! I knew it was too good to be true," said King Midas and he was so disappointed that he picked up a pebble to throw after the satyr.

The stone turned to gold in his palm.

"My wish! The satyr granted it after all!" cried Midas, and did a little dance on the spot. He ran to a tree and touched it. Sure enough, the twigs and branches turned to gold.

He ran back to his palace and stroked every wall, chair, table and lamp. They all turned to gold. When he brushed against the curtains, even they turned solid with a sudden clang.

"Prepare me a feast!" Midas commanded. "Being rich makes me hungry!"

The servants ran to fetch meat and bread, fruit and wine, while Midas touched each dish and plate (because it pleased him to eat off gold). When the food arrived, he clutched up a wing of chicken and bit into it.

Clang. It was hard and cold between his lips. The celery scratched his tongue. The bread broke a tooth. Every bite of food turned to gold as he touched it. The wine rattled in its goblet, solid as an egg in an egg cup.

"Don't stand there staring! Fetch me something I can eat!" Midas told a servant, giving him a push ... But it was a golden statue of a servant that toppled over and fell with a thud.

Just then, the queen came in. "What's this I hear about a wish?" she asked, and went to kiss her husband.

"Don't come near! Don't touch me!"

He shrieked, and jumped away from her. But his little son, who was too young to understand, ran and hugged Midas around the knees. "Papa! Papa! Pa—" Silence. His son was silent. The boy's golden arms were still hooped round Midas' knees. His little golden mouth was open, but no sound came out.

Midas ran to his bedroom and locked the door. But he could not sleep that night, for the pillow turned to gold under his head. He was so hungry, so thirsty, so lonely. So afraid. "Oh you gods! Take away this dreadful wish! I never realised!"

There was a clip-clopping of hoofs and the satyr put his head through the window. "I did try to tell you," he said.

Midas fell on his knees on the golden floor. His golden robe clanged and swung on him like a giant bell. His tall cap fell to the ground like a metal cooking pot. "Take it back! Please ask the gods to take back my wish!" he begged.

"With ears like that, I think you have troubles enough," said the satyr, laughing loudly. "Very well. Go and wash in the river. But do remember not to be so silly another time."

King Midas ran through the long grass, pushed his way through the long reeds, and leapt into the river. The ripples filled with gold dust, but the water itself did not turn to gold. Nor did the river bank as Midas pulled himself out. He was cured!

He carried
buckets of
water back
to the palace
and threw
them over
the little
golden statue
in the dining
room. And
there stood his
little son, soaked from head to foot and
starting to cry.

By this time, the grass had grown tall in the fields, and the reeds by the river were taller still. When the wind blew they rustled.

When the wind blew harder they murmured. When the wind blew harder still they whispered, "King Midas has long ass's ears!"

And on some windy days the reeds sang so loudly that everyone heard them for miles around: "King Midas has long ass's ears!"

And that is how King Midas' secret is known to us all today.